MW01014658

Lights, Camera, Action!

Adapted by Jim Fanning
Illustrated by Len Smith and Caroline Egan
Designed by Winnie Ho

A Random House PICTUREBACK® Book

Random House 🏠 New York

Copyright © 2008 Disney Enterprises, Inc. All rights reserved. Published in the United States by Random House Children's Books, a division of Random House, Inc., 1745 Broadway, New York, NY 10019, and in Canada by Random House of Canada Limited, Toronto, in conjunction with Disney Enterprises, Inc. Pictureback, Random House, and the Random House colophon are registered trademarks of Random House, Inc.

Library of Congress Control Number: 2008928064
ISBN: 978-0-7364-2550-6
www.randomhouse.com/kids/disney
Printed in the United States of America
10 9 8 7 6 5 4 3 2 1

Each week, fans of the action-packed television show *Bolt* tuned in to watch another adventure starring their favorite dog hero. They could hardly wait to see Bolt use his spectacular powers to keep his owner, Penny, safe from harm.

On the show, Penny's dad was a scientific genius. But Dr. Calico, the show's villain, was always trying to capture him and use his scientific inventions to do very bad things. To protect Penny, her father altered Bolt in his secret lab. With a **ZAP!**, the dog developed incredible powers.

In one episode, Calico captured Penny's dad. With Bolt by her side, the brave little girl set off on a daring rescue mission.

Penny soon discovered that the green-eyed villain wanted to capture her, too! But Calico had no plans for getting past . . .

. . . **Bolt!**

The amazing dog
would do anything to
protect Penny.

"Bolt, let's go!" Penny shouted as she hopped onto her scooter. **VRRROOM!** Penny and Bolt took off, racing to save her father. Bolt pulled the scooter down the street at an incredible speed.

Suddenly, helicopters roared overhead. A team of motorcyclists dropped down from one of them in hot pursuit. Calico's thugs were closing in on Bolt and Penny!

Just when it seemed as if Penny was going to be captured—**ZOOM!**—Bolt poured on the speed. The motorcycles could hardly keep up!

But then Bolt heard the unmistakable sound of one of Calico's choppers approaching. Using his heat vision, Bolt blasted the chopper and sent it crashing to the ground.

Then another chopper appeared! It hovered between Bolt and Penny, blocking Bolt's path. But that didn't stop him. Using his powerful legs, he leaped right over the spinning blades.

As soon as Bolt rejoined Penny—**WHOOSH!**—his mighty paws dug into the pavement. Bolt and Penny raced to safety. She smiled because nothing could get in their way now.

But Penny's smile quickly disappeared. Just ahead was a terrible sight. . . .

Dr. Calico's army was heading straight for them! How could Bolt stop Calico's troops? Penny knew just what her amazing dog could do to save the day.

"Bolt," Penny commanded. "Speak!"

Bolt prepared to unleash his secret weapon. Growling, the fearless dog faced the attackers and opened his mouth. **"RRRUUUFFFF!"**

The awesome force of Bolt's super bark sent Dr. Calico's powerful vehicles toppling backward as if they were toys.

Penny threw her arms around Bolt just as the episode came to an end.

Bolt fans would have to wait another week to find out if the heroic dog could save Penny's dad. But one thing was certain—Bolt loved Penny, and she loved him right back.